by Matthew K. Manning

illustrated by Joey Ellis

WHO TURNED OFF THE COLOURS?

raintree

a Capstone company — publishers for children

LEGEND SAYS . . .

The Rainbow-Barfing Unicorns
come from a faraway, magical
world called Pegasia. Not so
long ago, these stinky,
zombie-like, vomiting creatures
were banished to Earth for being,
well . . . stinky, zombie-like,
vomiting creatures. However,
Earth presents them with a new
danger: humans.

So, just who are the Rainbow-Barfing
Unicorns . . . ?

CHAPTER ONE

Mount Ashe looked angry on this particular Saturday. Not someone-ate-the-last-brownie angry. More like, I-shall-soon-belch-lava-all-over-your-tiny-town angry. It wasn't a good sign for Xander Stone's weekly magic show.

Xander could see the rather grumpy mountain from the performance stage. This was the part of his Rainbow-Barfing

Unicorn magic show where the three zombie unicorns – Cradie, Blep and Ronk – walked through the crowd.

With fresh make-up and a spritz of hairspray, the unicorns could skip right in front of visitors without anyone suspecting they were undead unicorns from the magical dimension of Pegasia. To the audience, the Rainbow-Barfing Unicorns were just miniature ponies in costumes, made to barf fake rainbows at the show's finale. No one suspected that they were looking at zombie unicorns in disguise – talking animals that would barf actual rainbows if they ate anything other than rubbish.

The problem was that during this part of the show, the Rainbow-Barfing Unicorns weren't sheltered under the stage's slanted roof. They were out amongst the crowd.

The storm giving Mount Ashe its angry appearance was an actual danger to Xander's friends. Not only would the audience be caught in the downpour, but so would the Rainbow-Barfing Unicorns. If their stage make-up washed off, their real identities would be revealed. And if that happened, authorities would surely drag them off to some government lab, secret medical centre or worse.

"Ladies and gentlemen," Xander said as he stepped off the stage, "we're having a bit of a weather issue." Just as Xander finished his sentence, a large raindrop splashed down on his nose.

"Boo!" came a roar from the audience.

The visitors hadn't come all the way

to the Montgomery Apple Orchard to pick apples or smell the stench of the neighbouring Henderson Landfill. They had come here to see Xander's show – and they weren't going to leave until they saw some magic.

"Um, well . . ." Xander began. "We're going to have to postpone–"

"Boo!" the audience roared again.

Then – *CRACK!* – a sudden crack of thunder boomed from behind Mount Ashe. A shadow fell over Xander's stage.

Xander looked up to see nothing but dark, cloudy skies. Then a few more raindrops smacked him in the face.

"–the show due to rain," Xander finished his sentence. "But we'll have another performance tomorrow afternoon at–"

"We want to see the rainbows!" shouted an angry man, who looked a little too old to be at a magic unicorn show.

Xander looked at the Rainbow-Barfing Unicorns. Several raindrops were landing on them now. Xander could even see a bit of Cradie's faded purple hide underneath her now splotchy make-up.

"OK, OK," Xander said. He now sounded less like the ringmaster of a professional stage show and more like a panicked twelve-year-old.

Xander rushed over to Cradie, Blep and Ronk. He pulled out three sticks of liquorice from his pocket and attempted to hand one to each of his unicorn friends. When Ronk ate all three pieces in one gulp, Xander rolled his eyes. Then he reached into his pocket for the spare liquorice he already knew he'd need. This wasn't his first unicorn rodeo, after all. Nearly everything that could go wrong in his magic show had gone wrong in countless past performances. He had a back-up plan for everything. Well, everything except for a crowd that would rather sit in the pouring rain than see their show cancelled.

Xander handed Blep a new piece of liquorice and then passed one to Cradie. Each unicorn quickly gobbled up the sweet.

Xander examined Blep as he chewed. The unicorn's make-up was dripping to the ground below him. Xander only hoped the audience couldn't see the Rainbow-Barfing Unicorns clearly through the pouring rain.

"And now, the moment you've all been waiting for!" Xander shouted into the crowd.

He pointed to the Rainbow-Barfing
Unicorns. Right on cue, they lived up
to their disgusting name.

"**CRADIE!**" Cradie brayed.

"**BLEP!**" Blep shouted.

"**RONK!**" Ronk ronked.

A beautiful beam of multi-coloured
light burst from each unicorn's mouth.
The beams shot through the air,
piercing through the
pouring rain.

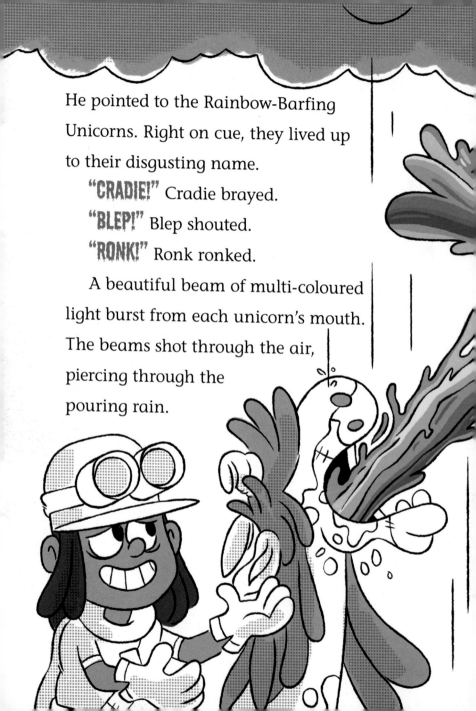

"Woo-hoo!" The audience stood and cheered.

Xander smiled and bowed with delight.

But when Xander glanced back at the Rainbow-Barfing Unicorns, his smile quickly vanished. The unicorns' make-up had almost completely washed away!

Xander rushed his friends off the stage and across the orchard's field. They knew they couldn't afford to be spotted without their make-up.

"That was a close one!" Xander said when they got to the unicorns' stables.

The Rainbow-Barfing Unicorns started to laugh.

And though Xander knew the situation could've been serious, he laughed too.

CHAPTER TWO

By morning, the sun returned. Several
puddles remained on the ground, especially
in the patch of earth behind the Rainbow-
Barfing Unicorns' stable. Depending on the
time of day, Cradie, Blep and Ronk liked
to rest in that patch and enjoy the shade
created by the stable's shadow. It was in this
shady, muddy place that Blep discovered
Ronk at around nine in the morning.

"RONK!"

Ronk had been ronking for the past hour. Even though Blep wasn't a morning unicorn, the sound woke him from the dirty mattress inside the stable. And if he had to be awake, then at least he could yell at his friend. Yelling was one of the small pleasures Blep enjoyed in life.

"What's with all the noise?" Blep yelled.

"Ronk," Ronk explained calmly.

As Blep had no idea what "ronk" meant, he walked over to his fellow unicorn and inspected the scene himself. Ronk had been munching on a packet of cookies he'd got from who knows where. ("Who knows where" was the usual source for all of Ronk's mysterious possessions.) It looked like the zombie unicorn was trying to barf a rainbow at the moment.

"**RONK!**" Actually, he wasn't trying to barf a rainbow – he was succeeding at it!

Usually when Rainbow-Barfing Unicorns barfed, they barfed into the air. The beautiful beam would light up the sky, creating quite a spectacle. It was no wonder people flocked to their show at the orchard every weekend.

Today, Ronk wasn't projecting light into the sky. He was aiming his mouth downwards, towards one of the mud puddles in the shady patch. The rainbow shot out from behind his crooked teeth and into the water. But instead of disappearing, as rainbows do, the colours stayed! The mud puddle itself had become a beautiful swirling pool of every colour in the spectrum.

"Whoa!" Blep gasped, despite himself. (He didn't mean to compliment his friend's work. After all, he still had more yelling to do.)

"Ronk," Ronk agreed, nodding his head. When Ronk's head shook up and down, Blep could hear something rattling around inside.

"How long does it stay like that?" Blep asked.

"Ronk," Ronk explained. The response meant nothing to Blep, but that was to be expected.

Ronk nodded his head towards the rest of the shady area, so Blep turned around. Behind him were several rainbow-coloured puddles. They were obviously the work of his friend's many morning ronks.

"Nice," Blep said, again accidentally complimenting the strange green unicorn.

Ronk smiled his crooked smile. He was proud of his accomplishments. He had made art – or at least a type of barfy art.

"Wow!" Cradie said as she rounded the corner of the stable. She had already noticed the puddles. "That's amazing!" she said to Ronk.

Ronk's smile widened.

"What a cool trick," Cradie said. "Don't let Xander see. He'll want to put that talent into our act."

That idea seemed to excite Ronk. Now he wasn't just a brilliant barf-artist, he was also a show designer!

"I wonder how long the puddles will stay like that?" Blep said.

CHAPTER THREE

Three hours later, the Rainbow-Barfing Unicorns were still wondering. . . .

In fact, they had been so occupied by the rainbow-swirling puddles, they nearly missed their next stage show. The audience had already been gathering in the nearby stands. The show would begin in less than thirty minutes – at twelve sharp!

Strangely enough, Xander was nowhere to be found.

"He's never late," Cradie said to Blep as the two wandered over to their "living room" at the Henderson Landfill. They lovingly referred to the area as Barf Central, which contained a few sofas, splintered coffee tables, a beanbag chair and plenty of rubbish to snack on.

"Ri row!" said Blep.

At the moment, Blep could barely speak. He had a paintbrush in his mouth and was doing his best to cover Cradie's faded purple skin with a thick coat of stage make-up. The job was usually Xander's, as he had two hands and absolutely zero hooves.

"It's just unlike him," said Cradie. "We can't have a show without our announcer."

"Ronk," Ronk agreed. He was bouncing on the nearby trampoline. Some of his make-up was already flaking off. Cradie and Blep weren't the artist Xander was.

Blep finished the coat of paint-like make-up. He took a step back to admire his work. He wished he hadn't. Cradie looked like a child's crude drawing of a unicorn, complete with splotchy colouring. Somehow, Blep had managed to colour outside the lines in real life.

Blep spit out the paintbrush in his mouth. "We need to find him," he said. "Let's go to his house."

"OK," Cradie said. She knew Blep didn't worry very often. "But how are we going to get there?"

■ ■ ■

Hitch-hiking is never a good idea –
who knows what kind of weirdo might
offer a lift. And that's if you're human!
Hitch-hiking is an even worse idea if you
happen to be a Rainbow-Barfing Unicorn.
But that didn't stop Cradie, Blep and Ronk
from trying.

The Rainbow-Barfing Unicorns stood
on the side of the road near the entrance
to the Montgomery Apple Orchard. They
had immediately attracted attention.
People took one look at their poorly
applied stage make-up and drove away.

To make matters worse, the Rainbow-
Barfing Unicorns obviously didn't have
thumbs. How were they expected to hitch
a lift when they couldn't even stick out the
one digit known to attract drivers? Trying

to hitch-hike without a thumb was like trying to use roller skates without human feet. And Cradie knew what she was talking about. She had tried both of those things.

After an hour with no luck, Cradie, Blep and Ronk decided that their best bet was to walk, even though that would take the best part of the day at their pace. (Or at Ronk's pace, anyway. He got distracted easily.)

However, as soon as they approached the first junction in the road, the Rainbow-Barfing Unicorns finally got lucky. In front of them was a large truck. It was standing still while the driver waited for the lights to change.

"Come on!" Cradie whispered as soon as she realized the opportunity.

Cradie rushed over to the truck, reared

back and then leaped directly into the truck bed. Her hooves barely made a sound. She crouched down in the back, so as not to be caught in the driver's rearview mirror.

"Huh," said Blep, impressed.

Not to be outdone, Blep reared back as well. He jumped right into the truck, nearly crashing into Cradie. His leap wasn't quite as graceful as hers, but it got the job done.

Outside the truck, Ronk paced around. The strange unicorn knew he couldn't jump as far as Cradie – or even Blep – but he didn't want to lose his friends.

Ronk took a step back. Just then, he noticed the truck's brake lights were no longer glowing red. The driver was about to pull away! (Even Ronk's scattered brain could work out that much.)

"C'mon, Ronk!" whispered Blep from the truck.

The truck slowly rolled forward.

Ronk looked both ways, as if he was about to cross a street. Then he ran towards the truck and jumped. . . .

WHAM! Ronk's front hooves were the only part of him that made the leap successfully. Blep and Cradie saw their fellow unicorn holding onto the truck bed for dear life as the vehicle turned a corner.

CHOMP! Blep bit onto one of Ronk's hooves. *CHOMP!* Cradie bit onto the other. They pulled as hard as they could. Ronk's back legs scraped against the back of the truck. The green unicorn tried desperately to find a foothold – or a hoofhold, as it were.

Cradie and Blep pulled harder.

Finally the trio felt themselves flying towards the front of the truck bed. They slammed into the back of the cab. It hurt, but Ronk was with them. They had managed to pull him out of harm's way!

Cradie, Ronk and Blep remained crouched down and out of sight. They were

all smiling, relieved to see Ronk safe.

Then Cradie felt something between her teeth. It tasted like a . . . jelly baby? It must have been stuck to Ronk's hoof. She swallowed it before even thinking twice. After all, when it comes to sweet treats, Rainbow-Barfing Unicorns don't have the greatest willpower.

As the truck drove down a hill towards Xander's neighbourhood, a bright rainbow shot out of its bed.

CHAPTER FOUR

A short while later, Cradie popped her head up. She recognized the tall evergreen trees that lined the road near Xander's house.

Cradie smacked Blep with her hoof. The hit was a little harder than she had intended.

"Hey!" Blep said.

"Jump!" was all Cradie said in response.

Then Cradie leaped out of the truck. Her hooves clunked against the asphalt of the road. Ronk followed without hesitation. Blep stole a glance at the driver of the truck, who was busy watching the road. Blep shrugged and then followed the other Rainbow-Barfing Unicorns.

The three unicorns trotted through the neighbourhood. Cradie remembered the way well enough. She had been here several times in Xander's bike trailer.

After turning onto a side street, the Rainbow-Barfing Unicorns found what they were looking for: Xander's little house at the base of a mountain.

When there was no sign of Xander in the front garden, the Rainbow-Barfing Unicorns tried the back garden. No Xander there, either. Cradie was beginning to worry that they'd passed him when they were huddled in the back of the truck. But her friends weren't ready to give up the search just yet. At the moment, both Blep and Ronk were pressing their entire faces against the back door, peering into Xander's kitchen.

"Guys!" shouted Cradie. "They'll see you!"

"Ain't that the point?" Blep said without moving.

"It's fine if it's Xander," said Cradie. "But we don't want to have to explain to his parents how we came all this way on our own."

"We'll just let Ronk explain it for us," said Blep.

"Ronk," Ronk agreed. (That would also

be his explanation, if pressed.)

Cradie rolled her eyes, but then curiosity got the better of her. She rushed over to the door, and added her face to the others currently crowding its window.

"There!" said Cradie. She nodded towards the living room.

The room was barely visible through the kitchen doorway. But the backs of two adult heads could be seen sticking up from behind the sofa. From the looks of it, Xander's parents were either watching TV or reading. Cradie couldn't be positive which.

"That's just the parents," said Blep.

"Right," said Cradie. "So where's Xander?"

"Ronk," suggested Ronk. (It wasn't the worst idea in the world.)

"Ronk's right," said Blep. He didn't

understand what his friend had said, but he at least wanted to let him participate.

"I think we should check Xander's room."

"Upstairs?" Cradie asked.

"Ronk," Ronk added.

Blep looked up at the roof. Then he said, "Too bad none of us is a Pegasus."

■ ■ ■

The garage door was open, and the ladder was inside. But that didn't make it any easier to carry. None of the unicorns could lift the ladder by themselves. When Ronk tried, the whole thing started to tip over. Cradie and Blep tried to dodge it, but the ladder fell straight over their heads.

Suddenly, all three of the Rainbow-

Barfing Unicorns looked more like Santa's reindeer than their usual selves. They were connected by the wooden "reins" of the ladder, each with his or her head through a hole between the rungs. As they couldn't look any more ridiculous, thanks to the awful stage make-up jobs they were still wearing, the Rainbow-Barfing Unicorns decided to just go with it. They walked around the house to the back garden. The ladder went with them.

With a lot of effort, the Rainbow-Barfing Unicorns propped the ladder against the house with a thud. Cradie peeked through the back door. Xander's parents hadn't heard the noise. Or if they had, they hadn't thought much of it.

Cradie hurried back to her friends. Blep was already halfway up the ladder.

"Careful," Cradie said.

Blep didn't answer. He was concentrating.
Climbing a ladder is a tricky thing for

unicorns. They can't exactly grip the rungs with their hooves. They can hold on a little bit with their teeth, but the slightest wrong move means disaster. And as Ronk didn't feel like waiting for Blep to finish his climb, if Blep fell, he'd take his friend down with him.

Finally, Blep's hooves touched the rooftop, and for the second time in as many minutes, he felt like one of Santa's reindeer. "I'm OK," he called down to his friends.

At the same time, Ronk decided he was in a hurry. The green unicorn jumped and skipped the last few rungs of the ladder, barely clearing the house's guttering.

"Ronk!" he said. His green face looked a bit paler than usual.

"You never did like heights," said Blep.

Ronk was too busy shaking to respond. Some of the dust and grime flaked off him and onto the roof tiles at his feet. Blep took a few steps back. He wasn't much cleaner than his fellow Rainbow-Barfing Unicorns, but he felt he should at least try to be.

"Oof," said Cradie. She had climbed the ladder in a hurry, although not quite as quickly as Ronk. She was either nervous about slipping, or wanted to make sure she didn't miss anything by being the last to arrive.

"So where's his room?" asked Blep. He was looking around the slope of the roof. There were no windows on this side.

Cradie walked past him and onto the opposite slope. From that point of view, she could see a small raised section of the house. At the end of it was a single window.

That was it – Xander's room!

Cradie was the first to look through the window. She was back in leader mode now. It was a natural role for her.

"I see–" she began.

"What?" said Blep. He pressed his nose against the glass over Cradie's shoulder.

"It's Xander," said Cradie. "But he's . . ." She couldn't bring herself to finish the sentence.

Inside the room, Xander lay in his bed. He had a comic book in his hands but looked like he was about to doze off to sleep. His eyes were barely open.

Even though comics usually entertained Xander more than any other form of entertainment, that wasn't the strange thing about him at the moment. Xander didn't look like his usual, colourful self. In fact, his skin was grey. His hair was a darker grey. Even his clothing was grey!

"He's . . . he looks like an old black-and-white film!" Cradie exclaimed.

CHAPTER FIVE

"Hey, Xander," Blep said as he slid the window open. He tried to step into Xander's room, but instead ran into the window's screen.

Xander jolted up in bed. He had almost been asleep. He wasn't sure if he was dreaming or if there were really three zombie Rainbow-Barfing Unicorns standing on his roof.

After a few seconds, he said, "Blep?"

Blep was rubbing his newly injured nose with his hoof. "Yeah?" he said. "I hate your window."

"Hold on!" Xander said. He was using a loud whisper now, suddenly aware of the situation. He jumped out of bed. He was wearing a bright purple onesie, but he was too worried to be embarrassed.

Xander clicked the metal tabs at the top and the bottom of the screen. Then he pulled the screen inwards and put it on the carpet in his room.

Blep jumped down into Xander's bedroom. He looked around and nodded. "Nice place," he said.

"How did you guys get here?" Xander

asked, ignoring Blep's compliment.

"More importantly, what is going on with your . . . colouring?" Cradie said as she landed on Xander's carpet with a muffled thud.

"Shh!" Xander said. "I don't want my parents to come up here."

"So explain why you look like the picture on that TV set Ronk found under a pile of cheese at the dump," said Blep.

"He means, why are you in black and white?" Cradie explains.

"I . . . ," Xander paused. "I'm not sure. If I had to guess, I'd say it's because of you."

"Me?" asked Cradie, insulted.

"Ronk," Ronk said as he fell through the window into the room. His thump was decidedly louder than Cradie's had been.

"Well, not you in particular," whispered Xander. "All three of you."

"You're gonna have to explain that one," said Blep.

"Mum and Dad have already taken me to the doctor this morning," Xander said. "As soon as they saw that I'd lost my colours. And they're not sure what's wrong with me. Well, not exactly."

"OK," said Blep, slumping down onto Xander's bed. Xander briefly wondered if his sheets would stink once Blep got up again. He knew the answer was yes.

"Well, they know one thing," said Xander. "They know I have a virus. A virus they've never seen before."

"An alien virus," Cradie said quietly.

"I think it's the same one that turned you guys into zombies," said Xander.

Everyone was quiet for a few moments.

"Ronk," said Ronk in a sad little bray.

No one disagreed.

CHAPTER SIX

"Everything OK up there, son?"
Xander's dad called from the bottom of
the stairs.

Xander's eyes went wide. "Hide," he
whispered. "You can't let my parents
see you."

"Xander?" Xander's dad called again.

"I'm fine, Dad!" Xander yelled in the
direction of his closed bedroom door.

His voice sounded anything but fine. So it came as no surprise to anyone in the room when they heard his dad's footsteps on the stairs below.

"Hide," Xander whispered again. Ronk scrambled up onto the top bunk and hid under the covers. Blep crammed himself under the bed. Cradie tried to do the same, but there just wasn't enough room.

"The wardrobe!" Xander said in a panicked voice.

Cradie sprinted to the wardrobe, but the door was closed. She tried the handle with her teeth, but couldn't pull hard enough.

Xander was in no position to help her either. He was in bed pulling his covers over himself. He needed to look as ill and innocent as possible.

The doorknob turned.

The door creaked.

Xander's eyes darted from it to Cradie, who stood frozen near the wardrobe. Cradie scanned the room. There was nowhere to hide, so she ran directly at Xander's bedroom door.

"Hey, kiddo," Xander's dad said as the door started opening.

WHUMP! The door suddenly stopped. Xander's dad furrowed his brow behind his thick glasses. "Huh?" he said, squeezing into the room.

"Hey, Dad!" said Xander excitedly. He sounded as if he hadn't seen his father for at least a month or two – certainly not just earlier this afternoon. "Look at this!"

Xander's dad gave up thinking about the door and walked over to his son's bunk bed. Wedged between the door and the wall, Cradie let out a tiny breath. She was doing her best not to make a sound.

"What have you got there?" Xander's dad asked.

"This awesome comic book!" said Xander. His distraction seemed to be working. He held up the comic in his hands and pushed it into his dad's face.

"You feeling OK, son?" asked his dad.

"Sure!" said Xander. "I mean, I'm black and white, but otherwise, I'm OK."

"Your comic book is upside down."

"Oh," said Xander. "Yeah, I like reading them that way. It makes the stories more exciting."

"Exciting?" his dad wondered aloud.

"Yeah, not only do they have to fight the bad guy, but they have to do it while hanging from the ceiling!" Xander said. He was making this all up. He wasn't even making sense to himself.

"Right," said his dad.

"How will they do it? How will they defy gravity and the odds?!" Xander was shouting now. He was getting carried away with this ridiculous excuse. He was hoping his dad would interrupt him soon.

Somebody needed to stop this, that was for sure!

"I think you need to get some sleep," said his dad. "The doctor wants to see you tomorrow afternoon. Your mum had a hard time convincing him to even let us bring you home. That means you need to take it easy."

"I'm sort of hungry," Xander said.

"Yeah? Shall I order us a cheese pizza?"

"Too spicy," Xander replied.

His dad looked at him. Like every kid in America, Xander had never turned down pizza. And since when was a plain cheese pizza spicy?

"Maybe I'll just have some crust?" added Xander after thinking it over.

"Ronk," said Ronk from under the covers.

"What was that?" Xander's dad asked.

"I said 'OK'," said Xander.

"It sounded like you said 'Ronk'," said Xander's dad.

"I added too many letters to it," said Xander.

Xander's dad wasn't really listening to his son at this point. He was busy smelling the air. He gave Xander a suspicious look. Finally, he said, "We need to change your sheets soon."

Xander just looked at him.

"It stinks in here," his dad said. He patted Xander on the head and walked out of the room, closing the door behind him.

Cradie collapsed to the floor. She was exhausted from pressing herself as flat as possible against the wall. "Take a little longer next time, why don't you?" she joked.

"Sorry, I–" Xander started to say when Blep interrupted him.

"Did you see his feet?" Blep said.

"Whose feet?" asked Xander.

"Your dad's, kid," said Blep. He slid out from under the bed. "I could see 'em as clear as day from under there."

"What are you talking about?" asked Xander.

"Your dad was walking around barefoot," said Blep.

"Yeah, so?" Xander didn't understand.

"His feet were grey, Xander," said Blep. "He's turning black and white too."

CHAPTER SEVEN

Xander immediately sprinted to the window and slid down the ladder. As they had discovered earlier, the Rainbow-Barfing Unicorns weren't meant to travel via ladder. Cradie, Blep and Ronk took nearly twice as long to get down.

But once Xander's feet touched the grass, he still showed no signs of slowing down.

"Xander!" Cradie called after him as she followed him to the street.

As soon as Cradie had yelled, she realized it was a mistake. It would be bad enough if someone saw her chasing after Xander so far away from her stable at the Montgomery Orchard. That would be pretty difficult to explain. It would be much worse if someone actually heard her speak. There'd be no explanation for that.

In either case, Xander didn't answer. He just kept running away from his house further down the street. Cradie kept galloping after him.

"Ronk!" she heard behind her.

Cradie glanced back and could see both Blep and Ronk following. They looked to be gaining on her, despite the fact that Ronk was running in a zigzag pattern. She hoped her rather odd unicorn friend didn't run into a garden fence – or worse, one of Xander's neighbours!

Xander got to the end of his street and turned. Cradie rolled her eyes. How much running was this day going to include?

As it turned out, not much more . . .

When Cradie rounded the corner, she nearly ran straight into her human friend. Xander had stopped at the edge of a garden and was staring at a house Cradie recognized. They had been there before. In fact, this was where the Rainbow-Barfing Unicorns had made their public debut as show "ponies". This was the house of the girl Xander had a crush on. This was where his friend Kelly lived.

"Xander!" Cradie whispered.

He didn't reply.

"What are we doing here?" Cradie continued.

Xander was out of breath. That was clear. He was huffing and puffing so much, it was as if he'd only just realized that he had been running. So again, he didn't respond. But to be fair, he would have been lucky to squeeze a single word out in the state he was in.

Cradie heard a noise coming from behind Kelly's house. Without hesitating, she dived behind a nearby hedge. Xander stood frozen in his tracks. He was a black-and-white statue, as if sculpted by an artist.

"Xander!" Cradie whispered.

The statue didn't move. The voices behind the house got louder. Cradie was pretty sure Xander didn't want his entire neighbourhood seeing him in black and white. So she jumped back up. She dug her unicorn horn right underneath his shoelaces, and then pulled her friend down to the ground.

After she had pulled Xander back behind the hedge with her, the boy finally spoke. "Thanks," he whispered, through a few huffs and puffs.

"Come into the sunlight where I can get a better look at you," came a familiar voice from nearby.

It was Kelly's Aunt Melinda, the owner of the Montgomery Apple Orchard. Cradie wasn't sure why Aunt Melinda was in Xander's neighbourhood and not at work.

But when she and Kelly stepped into the sunlight near the front of the house, it all became obvious.

"What is happening to us?" Kelly asked her aunt. Her eyes were big and a little wet. She looked extremely worried. Cradie thought she had every right to be. Because both Aunt Melinda and Kelly had lost their colour!

"This is all my fault," Xander whispered.

Cradie looked at her black-and-white friend and then back at the two other grey-toned humans near the house. She knew the boy was wrong. It wasn't his fault.

The blame fell squarely on her own shoulders.

CHAPTER EIGHT

The walk-in cupboard in Xander's basement seemed smaller than the last time they had used it. Blep, Cradie and Ronk all rested there on the ground, on the horrible One Trick Pony cartoon sheets that Xander claimed belonged to his sister. The more Cradie thought about it, the more she had her doubts. Someone had clearly written "Property of Xander" on the washing label.

The Rainbow-Barfing Unicorns had been hiding in Xander's basement since the day before. It had been raining again for the last few hours of the morning. Even if Xander wanted to risk being seen in black and white out in public, he certainly wasn't willing to cycle all the way to Henderson in the downpour.

"There's got to be a solution somewhere," Xander said.

"There's gotta be a bigger cupboard somewhere," Blep joked.

Xander ignored him and paced around.

"All this pacing and worrying isn't going to solve anything," said Cradie. "Let's just relax." Thinking about Aunt Melinda's office, Cradie added, "Don't you have a TV down here?"

Television was quite a treat for the Rainbow-Barfing Unicorns. They didn't have such a thing on Pegasia, and they certainly didn't have a TV in their stable at the orchard. If nothing else, Cradie knew the TV would do wonders for calming her own nerves. A good distraction might even help Xander.

Xander thought it over. "Hold on," he said, and walked off.

He was gone for what seemed like an hour to Cradie. Blep was complaining, Ronk was moaning and she was feeling a little cramped in the tight space. (In reality, Xander was gone for less than three minutes.)

When Xander returned, he carried a large box nearly half his size. It was a television set, Cradie realized upon further inspection.

It just wasn't the type of flat screen TV Xander had upstairs in the living room. This dusty old thing looked like it was state of the art . . . back in 1987.

A large orange cord trailed from the back of the TV. "I plugged in the extension over behind the washing machine," Xander said to the Rainbow-Barfing Unicorn, as if those words meant anything to magical unicorns from Pegasia.

"Great," said Blep. He didn't seem to mean it.

Xander pushed a button underneath the dusty screen, and then wiped the dust away as best he could. He made three clean stripes across the length of the screen until he gave up the effort and found a seat on the floor near Ronk.

Ronk dropped his head onto Xander's lap. Xander sighed. There went another pair of perfectly clean shorts. They were now coated in zombie unicorn filth. Oh well. He wasn't really a fan of grey clothing anyway.

The television buzzed to life. Cradie watched as a picture formed on the screen seemingly out of nowhere. Even on this hulking outdated machine, TV was magical to a unicorn.

". . . eye on your neighbourhood. Channel 4 News!" the TV was saying.

"Great," said Xander. "The news." He sighed again. Cradie was surprised how much Xander sounded like Blep at the moment.

"Then change the channel, please," said Blep.

"Can't," Xander responded without looking at his friend. "This thing only gets one channel."

"We begin this morning with breaking news from Henderson," said the blonde newsreader. For some reason she was smiling. It seemed inappropriate to Cradie, but then again, she wasn't a professional newsperson. "A strange presumed virus that affects pigment and, oddly enough, clothing, has caused a rash of sickness in the area, with reports of the illness stretching as far as many surrounding cities."

"Oh no," Xander said under his breath.

"We now go live to Corey Hughes in the centre of Henderson," said the woman.

The image changed to a young man standing in town, holding an umbrella.

Strangely enough, it didn't seem to be raining any longer. A few people could be seen talking on the pavement in the background.

"Look at them!" Xander said. He leaned forward towards the TV and tapped on the screen, hard. "There!"

Cradie squinted. It was hard to see in the less-than-ideal picture of the old television set, but Xander was right to be so worried. All the people milling about in the background were in black and white while the reporter was most definitely in colour. The people in the background seemed to be munching on something from a large brown sack. Cradie at first thought they might be eating raw potatoes, but that didn't make any sense.

"I can't believe it's spreading like this!" Xander said.

"I can," said Blep. "I mean, think about it. How many people have we entertained with our 'magic' show? Some of 'em got pretty close to us. Just makes sense they caught the virus if it's contagious to humans."

Xander turned around and looked at Blep.

"Well the good news is," Cradie said through a broken smile, "at least it's stopped raining."

Xander examined the TV. The reporter was lowering his umbrella as he talked.

"OK," Xander finally said after thinking for a few minutes. "Let's get you guys back to the dump."

Blep, Cradie and Ronk all stood up. Ronk stretched.

Then he shook out his mane. Mud, hair and what looked like a half-eaten lollipop now decorated the room.

"But first, I'm gonna need to make a stop in the kitchen for breakfast," Xander said.

"Sounds good to me," said Blep. "Could you grab us something too?"

"Absolutely," said Xander. "How do you feel about boiled beetroot?"

CHAPTER NINE

Xander and the Rainbow-Barfing
Unicorns sat in the woods behind his house,
sharing a plate of boiled beetroot. The
Rainbow-Barfing Unicorns had never tried
beetroot before, but they were certain that
Xander had overcooked them.

"Are these supposed to have, like, I don't
know . . . flavour?" Blep asked. Then he
turned his head to the side. "Blep!" he called

as a rainbow burst through the woods and into the otherwise grey sky.

Xander didn't answer. He had a beetroot in his hand, eating it like an apple.

"Butter would do wonders for these," said Cradie, before adding, "Cradie!" Another rainbow ripped through the tree line.

"Ronk!" Ronk agreed. His was both a response and a rainbow eruption.

 Xander was too busy working on his fifth beetroot to think anything of it.

"Seriously," said Blep. He walked away from his half-eaten beetroot and found a nice, partially dry rock to sit on. "What's next, boiled potatoes? Or how about some equally flavourless tofu to liven things up?"

Xander finally took a break from furiously devouring his breakfast. "Do you have any boiled potatoes?" he asked. His eyes were wide with excitement.

Cradie and Blep exchanged looks.

"How about your favourite?" said Cradie. "A nice tart green apple."

"The virus did come with cravings," Blep said to Cradie. He was talking to her as if Xander wasn't even there. The way Xander was chomping on his sixth beetroot, he might as well not have been.

"But boiled potatoes?" Cradie said.

"Do you have any boiled potatoes?" Xander repeated, more anxious and excited than last time.

"Um, no," Cradie was saying. But Xander wasn't listening. He had darted out of the woods and was already at his house's back door.

"This is bad," Blep said, watching the black-and-white boy dash inside.

Cradie exhaled loudly. She looked at Blep with concern. Then she glanced over at Ronk. He didn't seem particularly worried at the moment. In fact, he was smiling. He had found a puddle the perfect size for his continued experiments.

"Ronk!" he brayed as a rainbow shot from his mouth into the muddy water. As before, the rainbow stayed in place in the shallow pool. It glimmered in the shadows of the trees, like a magical – yet disgusting– oasis.

Cradie sighed even louder. Then she heard a scream from inside Xander's house.

"Yes!" a woman's voice exclaimed. "That's a great idea!"

Just that second, Xander raced back out of the door and into the little forest.

"It's on!" he yelled as he got closer. He stumbled into the tree line again, saying, "Mum's making boiled potatoes right this second! She's really excited about it!"

"Is she black and white too?" Cradie asked.

"Huh?" said Xander. Then he added, "You know, I didn't notice."

Blep stepped forward, about to speak. But unfortunately, at that exact moment, Xander began pacing again, looking back at Cradie as he walked.

"I can't wait until we–" Xander began. But he never finished his sentence.

Instead, Xander tripped over Blep's back and stumbled towards Ronk. Ronk jumped out of the way, clearing the path so Xander landed face first in the newly formed rainbow puddle.

"Xander!" Cradie yelled.

"Ronk," Ronk said in a sad little voice. He had worked very hard on that particular piece of "artwork".

Xander leaned backwards and shook his head, splattering rainbow-dyed drops of water on several nearby trees. "I'm OK," he said after catching his breath.

"You're more than OK," Cradie said from her now-gaping mouth.

Blep cracked his aching back and then peered up at Xander. "Whoa," he said quietly.

"What?" Xander said.

The Rainbow-Barfing Unicorns were too amazed to tell the boy that his colours were back!

CHAPTER TEN

The tyres on the bike's trailer squeaked as Xander wheeled his bike through the town of Henderson. He had got a bit too tired of pedalling the weight of the three zombie unicorns hiding under a blanket in the trailer. About ten minutes ago, he'd hopped off his seat and was now taking a break as he pushed his bike along the pavement.

He had successfully regained his breath.

But that wasn't what he was worried about. Xander was hoping no one in the town realized that he was the only person who had any colour at all.

On his right, two black-and-white women wearing drab, grey police uniforms were arguing over something. Xander couldn't tell what it was without steering his bike closer to them, an action he was not willing to take.

To Xander's right, three grey-toned kids were snacking on raw beetroot. They seemed as happy as if they had just flagged down an ice cream van. Xander shuddered. His belly still ached from all the boiled beetroot he had devoured earlier. Now that he had regained his colouring, he wasn't anti-beetroot, he just thought they should either be buttered or pickled if people were going to eat them.

The cravings he had suffered while sick with the alien virus were gone. Now he wanted nothing more than a tall glass of lemonade. Very flavourful lemonade, if possible.

"*Psst . . .*" Blep whispered from under the blanket. "How's it looking out there?"

"Bad," Xander said, not bothering to whisper. As it turned out, no one was paying him any attention. All that the people in Henderson cared about were beetroots and potatoes.

"Cradie's got an idea," Blep whispered.

At that, Xander wheeled the bike towards a patch of unoccupied grass at the start of the small city park. There, in the shade of a tree and safely away from any beetroot-obsessed townspeople, Xander could talk freely with the Rainbow-Barfing Unicorns without anyone overhearing them.

"OK," said Xander. "What's the plan?"

Cradie popped her head out of the blanket. "The reservoir," she said. "We fill up the city's water supply with rainbows. That way we can cure the whole town in one swoop."

"OK," Xander said again. "So where's the reservoir?"

"I don't know," said Cradie. "You're the human."

"Won't they have, like, security there?" Xander asked.

"Probably," said Cradie.

"So how do we get past them?" Xander asked. "I mean, I'm a boy and you're three Rainbow-Barfing Unicorns."

"You're making this plan sound difficult," said Cradie. She wasn't happy that Xander was being the party pooper.

"Because I think it is difficult," he said.

Cradie hung her head.

"Hey, you got any better ideas?" Blep asked. He stuck his head out from under the blanket as well. The blanket fell behind the trio of unicorns and into the grass.

Xander looked around. No one was noticing these unicorns with their all-but-wiped-off stage make-up. The only humans around were an elderly couple gnawing on raw potatoes. The old man seemed to be having the hardest time of it. He removed his potato from his mouth, and his set of dentures came out with it. His wife frowned at him.

Xander shrugged. There didn't seem to be a point in hiding his unicorn friends any longer.

Which was fortunate, because Ronk had no intention of staying hidden. The unstable unicorn jumped out of the back of the trailer and trotted over to one of the park's outdoor barbecues. Xander and the rest of the Rainbow-Barfing Unicorns watched the unicorn with curious expressions.

"Ronk," Xander said. "Come on. Get back here. We don't have time to play."

But Ronk wasn't interested in playing. He leaned down and gripped the pole-like base of the barbecue with his broken teeth. Then he shook it vigorously. Grey ash instantly coated Ronk and the grass around him. As if he had just solved all the world's problems,

Ronk strolled proudly back to Xander, Cradie and Blep. He smiled his crooked smile and waited for a response.

"What is wrong with you?" Xander said. "It's going to take forever to hose you off."

"Too bad it's not raining any more," Blep said, almost to himself.

Then Cradie's eyes went wide. She looked from Blep to Xander. "That's what Ronk's trying to say!" she almost shouted.

"Ronk," Ronk said. He gave a knowing nod.

"Ash," said Xander. As if prompted, thunder cracked in the distance. Xander titled his head toward the towering mountain beyond the town. Another huge storm cloud was forming behind it. "Mount Ashe," Xander said, finally getting it.

"We don't need to rainbow the water supply," said Cradie. "We need to rainbow the clouds themselves."

Xander and all three Rainbow-Barfing Unicorns looked towards the intimidating mountain.

"Ronk," Ronk said in a quiet voice.

CHAPTER ELEVEN

Xander and the Rainbow-Barfing Unicorns had gone as far as the road could take them. He looked up, but there wasn't much to see. Just a stretch of forest past a wire fence that clearly read: No Trespassing. It was hard to tell they were even at the base of Mount Ashe. It was just a steep hill from this vantage point, one that showed no signs of stopping as it disappeared into cloud-like plumes of mist.

Thunder crashed, bringing Xander back to reality.

"The storm's going to pass completely if we don't get a move on," Cradie said.

She and the rest of the Rainbow-Barfing Unicorns were out of the bike's trailer now. They hadn't seen a human being other than Xander for at least fifteen minutes. Mount Ashe wasn't really a tourist attraction, so the unicorns had no fears of being discovered.

Xander wheeled his bike and trailer to a nearby ditch. They couldn't be spotted from the road there. The deep trench should serve as enough cover. He reached into the trailer and pulled out a small, roundish object. He put it in his pocket.

Better safe than sorry.

"There's no turning back now," Xander said.

It was quiet there near the country road. Only the sound of a dog barking in the distance could be heard over Xander climbing the tall wire fence that separated the forest from the road. After at least five minutes of pure, unfit effort, Xander had conquered the fence. He fell to its other side with a thud. He gave the concerned Rainbow-Barfing Unicorns a thumbs-up from his position on the ground.

Cradie was next. With a scuttling of hooves and rotten teeth, she made her way up the fence. She leaped gracefully down to the ground near Xander. Blep did the same.

But when they looked for Ronk to see if he was following, there was no sign of the weird little green unicorn.

"Ronk!" came a voice directly behind Xander. He jumped, before realizing who it was that was ronking. It's not like the list of suspects was very long.

"How did you–" Xander began as his eyes drifted to the fence behind Ronk. There he saw a Ronk-size hole cut neatly in the wiring. It was as if it had been eaten away by a particularly odd zombie unicorn. "Oh," Xander said under his breath. "Great." He was going to have to send some money to whoever owned this property.

Xander was already uneasy about the idea of trespassing. But property damage was too much for him. He wondered how many weeks of Rainbow-Barfing Unicorns shows it would take to pay for a new section of wire fencing.

Without another word, Xander and his friends began to hike up the mountain and into the forest. They were all too nervous to notice that the sound of the barking dog was getting louder.

CHAPTER TWELVE

"Stop right there!" shouted a deep voice
from the woods.

Xander and the Rainbow-Barfing
Unicorns had been walking for about an
hour when they heard the man yelling
at them. The young boy certainly hadn't
expected to see any other hikers this far up
the mountain.

Xander turned to see a man armed with a shovel. The shovel seemed an odd accessory, but Xander didn't think much about it in the heat of the moment. Behind the man was a very large brown dog. The beast seemed as big as a fully grown horse. It wasn't, but don't try telling Xander that.

"Um . . . hello?" Xander said.

"What the Sam Hill are you doing up on my property?" asked the man. Xander didn't know who Sam Hill was. He was in no hurry to find out.

"Just . . . just out for a walk," said Xander.

"Not up here you ain't," said the man. Now Xander was really confused. Of course they were. The man could see them for himself. This was exactly where they were walking. "Get going."

"Oh, uh, of course" said Xander. "But we were really hoping to reach the top of the mountain first, if that's not a problem." For the first time, Xander realized that this man was in black and white. It was hard to tell at first. Grey tones seemed to be a natural fit for this old-fashioned character.

"We?" said the man. "Who's we? Are there more of you kids out here?"

Xander realized he had been talking about his unicorns as if they were people, not ponies in costumes, as he wanted others to believe. One minute into a conversation, and he was already blowing his friends' secret identities.

"No," said Xander. "I misspoke. It's just me. Me and my . . . um, ponies."

"Enough blabbering, then," said the man. "Off my land. Now." There was no maybe in this man's voice. He was giving a direct order.

Xander locked eyes with Cradie. This wasn't going to work.

"And you were worried about guards at the reservoir," she whispered.

Then, without another word, she ran full speed at the strange man.

Using her horn, Cradie knocked the shovel right out of the man's hand. He yelped in surprise more than pain, but it was enough to anger his dog. The dog began barking at Cradie. Blep and Ronk rushed over to their friend, but the dog didn't back down. He snarled and showed his sharp fangs.

So the Rainbow-Barfing Unicorns did the same. They opened their mouths, revealing their rotten – and in some cases missing altogether – teeth. It might have been the sight of their unseemly chompers, or perhaps their breath, but something spooked the dog. He yelped louder than his master and then turned and ran away.

Unfortunately, the man wasn't as easily frightened. He picked up his shovel again and swung it at Cradie. She barely dodged the attack, narrowly escaping with her horn and head intact. He swung again at Blep. Blep leaped out of the way but collided with Ronk and Cradie in the process. All three unicorns fell to the ground, dazed.

The man stood over them. He raised his shovel for a final blow. And then something hit him square in the forehead.

The man looked at the ground through hazy eyes. As soon as they regained their focus, he could see that there was a raw beetroot lying on the grass near his work boots. His mouth fell open. His hands fell to his sides. The shovel fell to the ground with a harmless thud. Then the man pounced on the beetroot and began to chew it madly like a wolf that had happened upon a T-bone steak.

"Wha . . . ?" Blep said as he got to his hooves.

"Let's go!" shouted Xander. In no time at all, he and the Rainbow-Barfing Unicorns were rushing through the woods towards the mountain's peak.

CHAPTER THIRTEEN

Xander reached into his pocket. He was out of beetroot, but had the next best thing, gummy worms. He threw one to Ronk, one to Blep and one to Cradie. They swallowed the gooey sweets without even chewing. Then they titled their heads towards the massing rainclouds above.

"You can do it, guys," Xander said. He felt a raindrop land on his nose. Then another on his arm. "It's now or never," he added.

Three beams of beautiful, multicoloured light lit up the air there at the top of Mount Ashe. The light shot from the rock formation where the Rainbow-Barfing Unicorns stood into the huge grey clouds over their heads. The three rainbows hung in the sky. Beautiful, disgusting barf rainbows. Then they faded from view.

No one said anything for a few seconds.

Then Cradie broke the silence. "Did we do it?" she asked Xander.

"I don't know," Xander said.

As if in reply, another raindrop landed on him. Then another. Then another. Xander raised the back of his hand to his face. There, swirling and shimmering near his knuckles, were a few pools of water with a rainbow trapped neatly inside. Xander held out both of his hands. The rain was coming down heavier now. It took no time at all for him to catch a few more raindrops. Each was multicoloured and beautiful. He looked over at his unicorn friends, but they were busy splashing and playing in the rainbow rain.

■ ■ ■

The news of the cure to the black and white virus travelled quickly. An old couple had been caught in the rainstorm in town, and regained their colour in a matter of seconds. Before Xander and the Rainbow-Barfing Unicorns had even got back to their stable at the Montgomery Apple Orchard and Farm, the citizens of every town in a forty-mile radius were out

dancing in the street, making a rainbow
mess of their clothing and shoes. As he
sat in Aunt Melinda's office, watching
her TV, Xander was sure the crisis
had been averted. Their cure had
worked.

He and the Rainbow-Barfing Unicorns walked through the pouring rainbow rain back towards the Henderson Landfill. The Rainbow-Barfing Unicorns were hungry after their adventure, and needed a spot of rubbish-supper to tide them over until the next day. Blep and Ronk ran ahead, anticipating their dinner. But Cradie kept pace with Xander. She had something to say to him. Xander could tell that just by looking at her face. Unicorns were never good about keeping feelings to themselves.

"What's up?" he said when the other two unicorns were out of earshot.

"Nothing," she said. But then thought better of it. "I just don't get it," she said.

"Get what?"

"Well, we're the reason for the colour

loss, right? In the humans? I mean, we brought that alien virus here," she said.

"Yeah," said Xander. "Probably, I think."

"So if it was the same virus, then how come the rainbow rain didn't cure us too?"

Xander stopped in his tracks. He hadn't thought about that. Of course Cradie would want to be cured. No one could enjoy being a zombie. Were there any perks in a life of barfing rainbows?

"I don't know," said Xander. "But it obviously affected humans in a different way. Maybe it was a mutant strand or something that only worked on people. It's not like the virus ever hurt any other unicorns you guys knew in Pegasia."

Cradie hung her head low. "Yeah," she said. "Probably something like that," she said.

"I'm sorry, Cradie," Xander said.

The two walked through the gate to the Henderson Landfill. Before Cradie could say anything else, Ronk splashed a puddle of rainbow-coloured water at her face. She wiped the rain off. She still looked upset.

"Oh," said Blep. "Um . . . sorry about that."

Cradie's eyes narrowed, her nose crinkled. A slight smile appeared in the far corner of her mouth.

"It's on now!" she said before braying something not unlike a happy war cry.

Cradie charged at Blep, knocking him into a huge rainbow puddle. Xander opened his mouth to say something, but that was indeed a terrible idea. Because in the next instant, Xander was spitting out a mouthful of rainbow water, trying his best to stop laughing.

CHARACTER SPOTLIGHT:
XANDER!

Height: 1 metre 64 centimetres

Species: Human

Home planet: Earth

Horn length: N/A

Xander Stone is an average twelve-year-old. Well, actually, he WAS an average twelve-year-old . . . until he met the Rainbow-Barfing Unicorns. Now he's an average twelve-year-old with the responsibility of keeping Blep, Cradie and Ronk a secret from pretty much all other humans. Or the fate of the world could be at stake. No biggie.

GLOSSARY

banish send someone away from a place and order them not to return

contagious able to be passed on by contact between individuals

dimension place in space and time

distraction something that makes it hard to pay attention

landfill system of waste disposal in which the rubbish is buried between layers of earth

Pegasus winged horse from ancient-Greek mythology

reservoir artificial or natural lake where water is collected as a water supply

spectrum range of colours shown when light shines through water or a prism

BARF WORDS

blow chunks barf

heave barf

hork barf

hurl barf

puke barf

ralph barf

regurgitate barf

retch barf

spew barf

throw up barf

upchuck barf

vomit barf

yak barf

JOKES!!

What's black and white and
eats like a unicorn?

A zebra.

What kind of bow is
easiest for a Rainbow-
Barfing unicorn to tie?

A rain-bow!

Why was the
unicorn such a good
guitar player?

He knew the
uni-chords.

Do they have unicorns at the zoo?

Yes! They're just large, grey and called rhinos.

How do you know that a

unicorn has been in

your house?

There's glitter everywhere!

AUTHOR

The author of more than seventy-five books, Matthew K. Manning has written several comic books as well, including the hit *Batman/ Teenage Mutant Ninja Turtles Adventures* miniseries. Currently the writer of the new IDW comic book series *Rise of the Teenage Mutant Ninja Turtles*, Manning has also written comics starring Batman, Wonder Woman, Spider-Man, the Justice League, the Looney Tunes and Scooby-Doo. He currently lives in North Carolina, USA, with his wife, Dorothy, and their two daughters, Lillian and Gwendolyn.

ILLUSTRATOR

Joey Ellis lives and works in North Carolina, USA, with his wife, Erin, and two sons. Joey writes and draws for books, magazines, comics, games, big companies, small companies and everything else in between.